THE ORACLE'S TRINITY

Strength - Harmony - Hope

I0692167

BOOK 1: STRENGTH

The Oracle of Resilience, Growth, and Action

*Wisdom for those seeking
empowerment, breakthroughs, and momentum in life*

Written & Illustrated by K.J. Kilo

Book 1 of 3 in The Oracle's Trinity
Written & Illustrated by K.J. Kilo
Cover Design by K.J. Kilo

First Edition - 2025

ISBN: 979-8-9907041-1-4

Contents Guide

Origins

There exists sacred wisdom that freely flows through the ether of the universe, waiting for awakened souls to hear its calls. So vast is the wisdom that a single truth can shake the heavens, unravel existence, and forever alter the path of those who seek it.

For centuries, whispers of this wisdom surfaced in the verses of poets, the teachings of philosophers, and the silent knowing of the soul. Yet, its truths remained fragmented, like pieces of a great cosmic puzzle waiting to be assembled.

In time, those attuned to the echoes of this wisdom felt an unseen force drawing them together. They gathered in secret sanctuaries, forming an ancient order known as the Elokar. They sought to unite the scattered pieces of wisdom into complete sacred texts that could benefit mankind.

Ages passed, and the name of the Elokar faded into whispers; their sacred texts lost to time. Until a hidden cave, untouched for millennia, revealed their secrets once more. Among the forgotten scrolls and relics, three books shone brighter than the rest. Together, the books were called **Torielok Vaelen - The Three Sacred Pillars of Elokar**.

Their words, though ancient, still spoke to the hearts of those who sought wisdom and still held relevancy. Over generations, the wisdom of Torielok Vaelen was reborn, its essence distilled into a condensed form that speaks to all who seek its truths.

Today, this condensed form is known as **The Oracle's Trinity**, consisting of three books:

Book 1: Strength - The Oracle of Resilience, Growth, and Action

Book 2: Harmony - The Oracle of Love, Inner Peace, and Purpose

Book 3: Hope - The Oracle of Courage, Vision, and Infinite Possibilities

Book Structure

Book 1: Strength - The Oracle of Resilience, Growth, and Action is the first volume of The Oracle's Trinity. It serves as a powerful guide for those seeking empowerment, breakthroughs, and the momentum to transform their lives.

This book is divided into three **Oracle Categories**, each containing nine verses, for a total of 27 verses:

1) Resilience and Overcoming Challenges
   (Guidance on enduring hardship)

2) Growth and Self-Discovery
   (Evolving into one's highest self)

3) Motivation and Action
   (Inspiration to move forward)

Each verse is presented as a two-page spread, spanning both the left-hand (verso) and right-hand (recto) pages. This structured format includes three key elements: a **quote**, a **reflection**, and the **Whispers of the Oracle**.

Three Elements of Each Verse

- Quote - The Sacred Wisdom
  A powerful statement or excerpt that embodies a timeless truth.

- Reflection - Expanding the Wisdom
  A deeper exploration of the quote's meaning, offering insight, guidance, and perspective to help the reader internalize and apply its message.

- Whispers of the Oracle - A Poetic Journey
  A poetic expression of the Sacred Wisdom, designed to evoke emotion and deepen your connection to its truth.

How to Use This Book

The 27 verses from the three Oracle Categories are woven together in random order to provide an intuitive experience. There is no wrong way to seek its wisdom.

You may choose to follow the book in order, or you can simply open to a random page and let the verse you find be the wisdom you need for the day. You might read one verse at a time or several in a single sitting - the choice is yours.

If you're drawn to a specific Oracle Category, turn to the **Thematic Guide** (page 55) to quickly locate the verses for each category.

At the end of the book, you'll find a dedicated "Notes" section - a space to capture your thoughts, reflections, insights, or even sketches as you journey through this book.

There are many paths through a forest; similarly, there are many ways to seek wisdom. Choose your own path as you uncover the knowledge within **The Oracle's Trinity**.

The Oracle's Message

Before the mountains stood and the rivers carved their paths, strength was written into the fabric of all things. The stars burn with it, the earth hums with it, and within you, it has always existed—waiting to awaken.

Strength is not the absence of struggle but the mastery of it. It is the fire that refuses to be extinguished, the roots that grow deeper in the storm, the warrior who rises even when weary. These verses do not teach you how to become strong—they remind you that you already are.

As you turn these pages, do not seek answers as though they are lost. The wisdom of resilience, growth, and action has been woven into your very soul. These words will only help you remember.

May this book be your compass in uncertain times, your whisper in the silence, and your flame in the dark.

The path before you is yours to claim—walk it boldly

GROWTH & SELF DISCOVERY
Evolving into one's highest self
Verse 9

"The journey within is the greatest adventure you will ever take"

Reflection:

Self-discovery is a transformative process, unlocking wisdom, strength, and purpose.

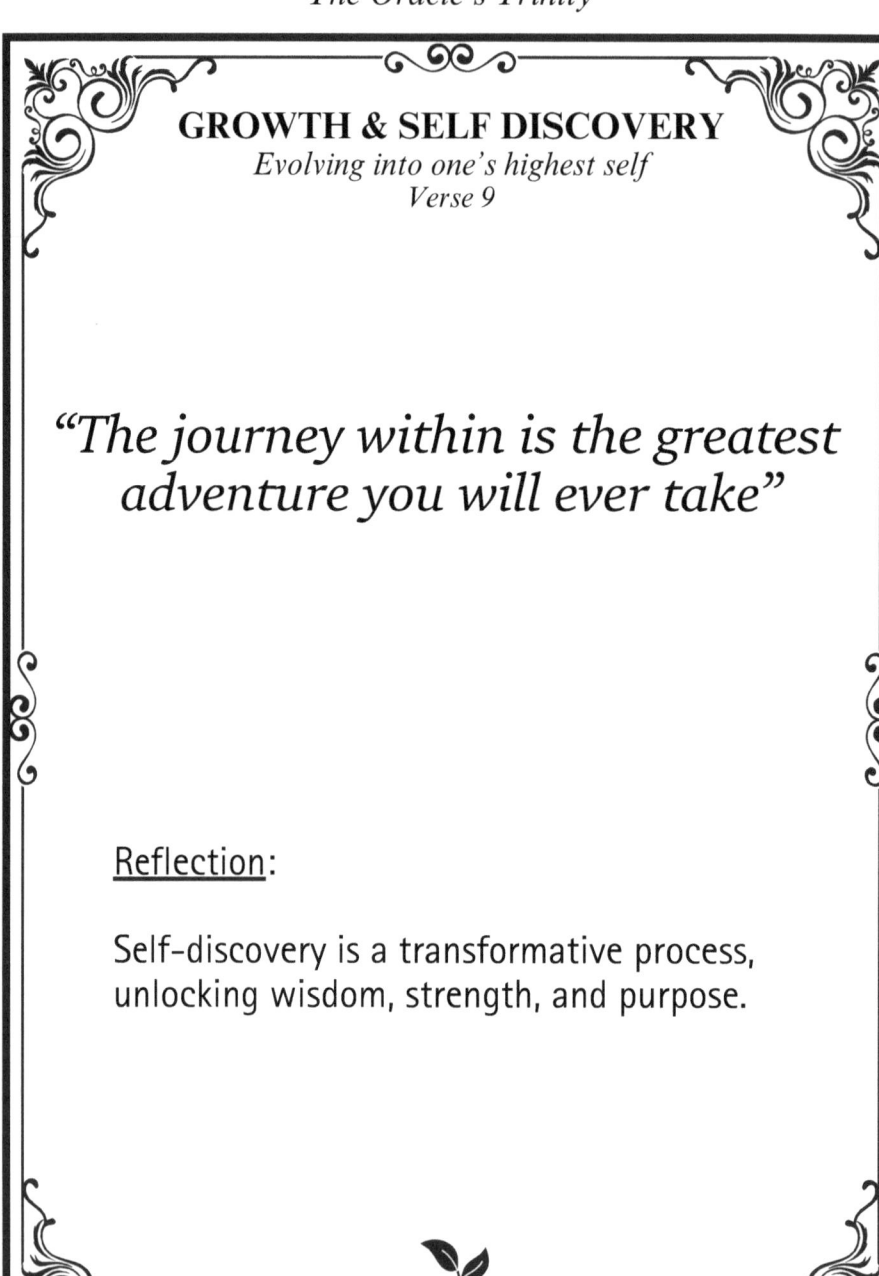

GROWTH & SELF DISCOVERY
Evolving into one's highest self
Verse 9

Whispers of the Oracle

A journey inward, vast and grand,

A world unseen, yet close at hand.

Explore, reflect, and you will find,

the greatest treasures of the mind

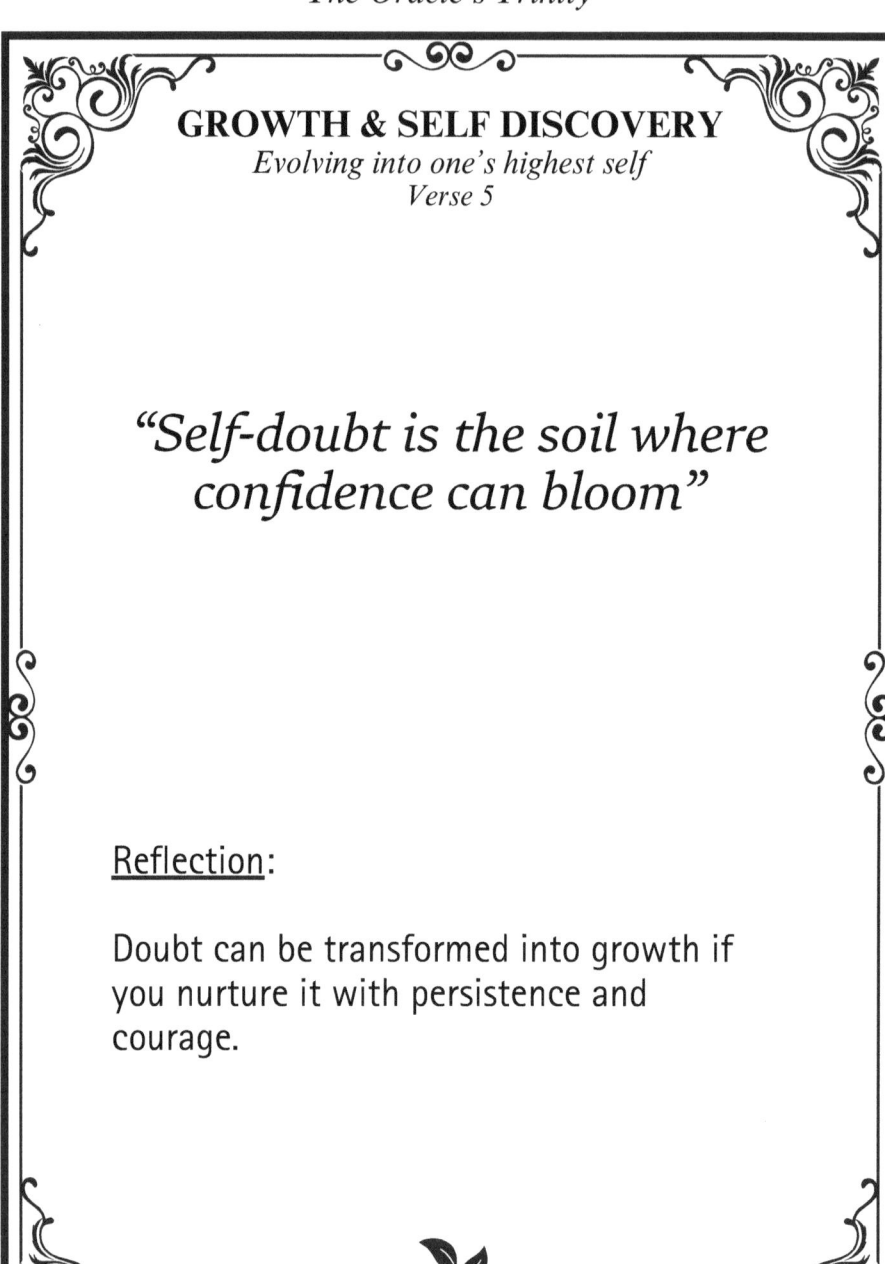

GROWTH & SELF DISCOVERY
Evolving into one's highest self
Verse 5

"Self-doubt is the soil where confidence can bloom"

Reflection:

Doubt can be transformed into growth if you nurture it with persistence and courage.

GROWTH & SELF DISCOVERY
Evolving into one's highest self
Verse 5

Whispers of the Oracle

From doubt's dark earth, a sprout will rise,

A bloom of strength beneath the skies.

Water it well, let hope take root,

Confidence grows where fear is mute.

MOTIVATION & ACTION
Inspiration to move forward
Verse 6

"Procrastination is the thief of time - act now and reclaim it"

Reflection:

Delays steal opportunities. Act decisively and reclaim control of your future.

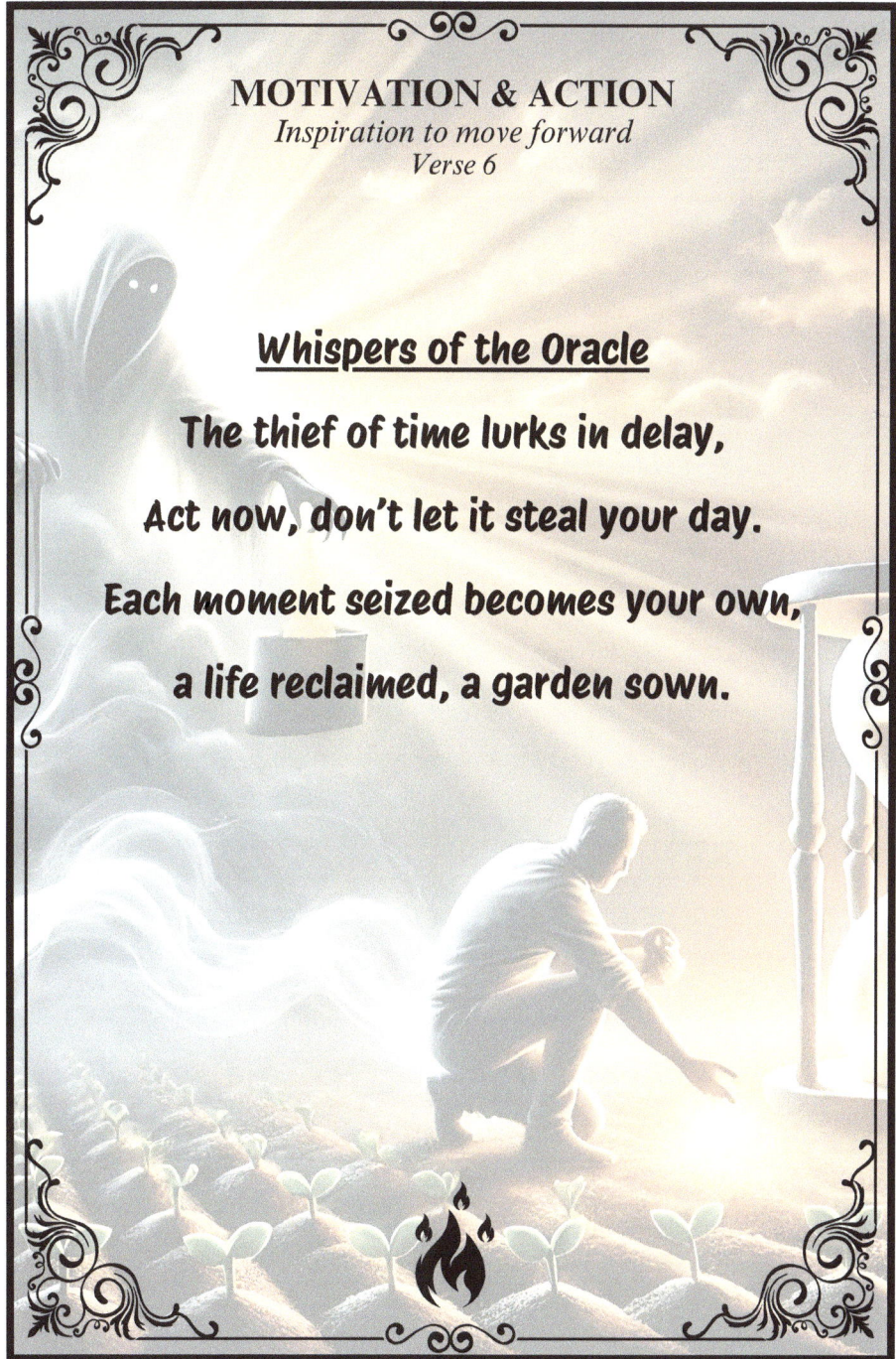

MOTIVATION & ACTION
Inspiration to move forward
Verse 6

Whispers of the Oracle

The thief of time lurks in delay,

Act now, don't let it steal your day.

Each moment seized becomes your own,

a life reclaimed, a garden sown.

RESILIENCE & OVERCOMING CHALLENGES
Guidance on Enduring Hardships
Verse 3

"Fear is the shadow of courage - walk through it to find the light"

Reflection:

Fear often masks your inner strength. By confronting it, you unlock the courage hidden within.

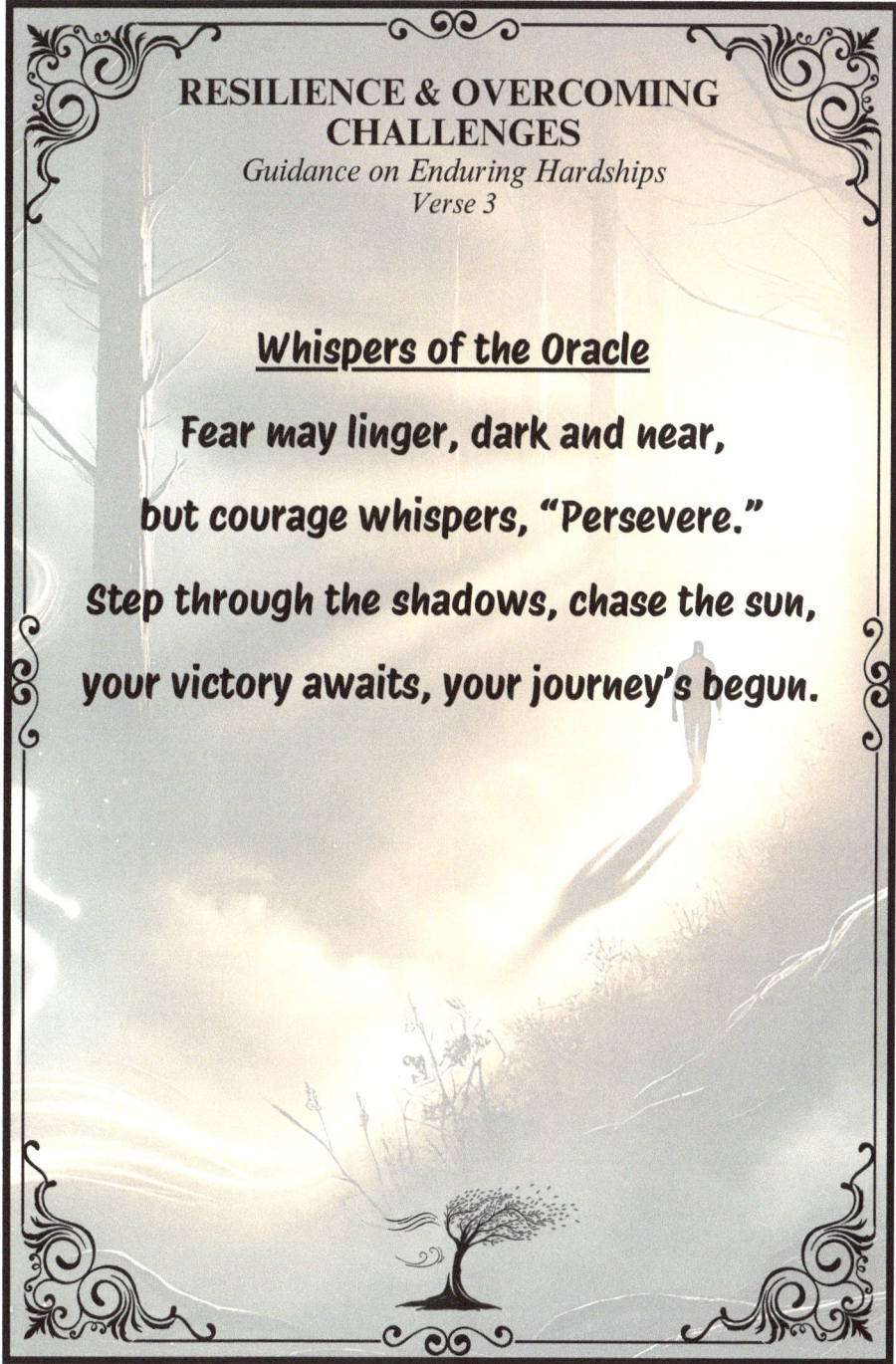

RESILIENCE & OVERCOMING CHALLENGES
Guidance on Enduring Hardships
Verse 3

<u>Whispers of the Oracle</u>

Fear may linger, dark and near,

but courage whispers, "Persevere."

Step through the shadows, chase the sun,

your victory awaits, your journey's begun.

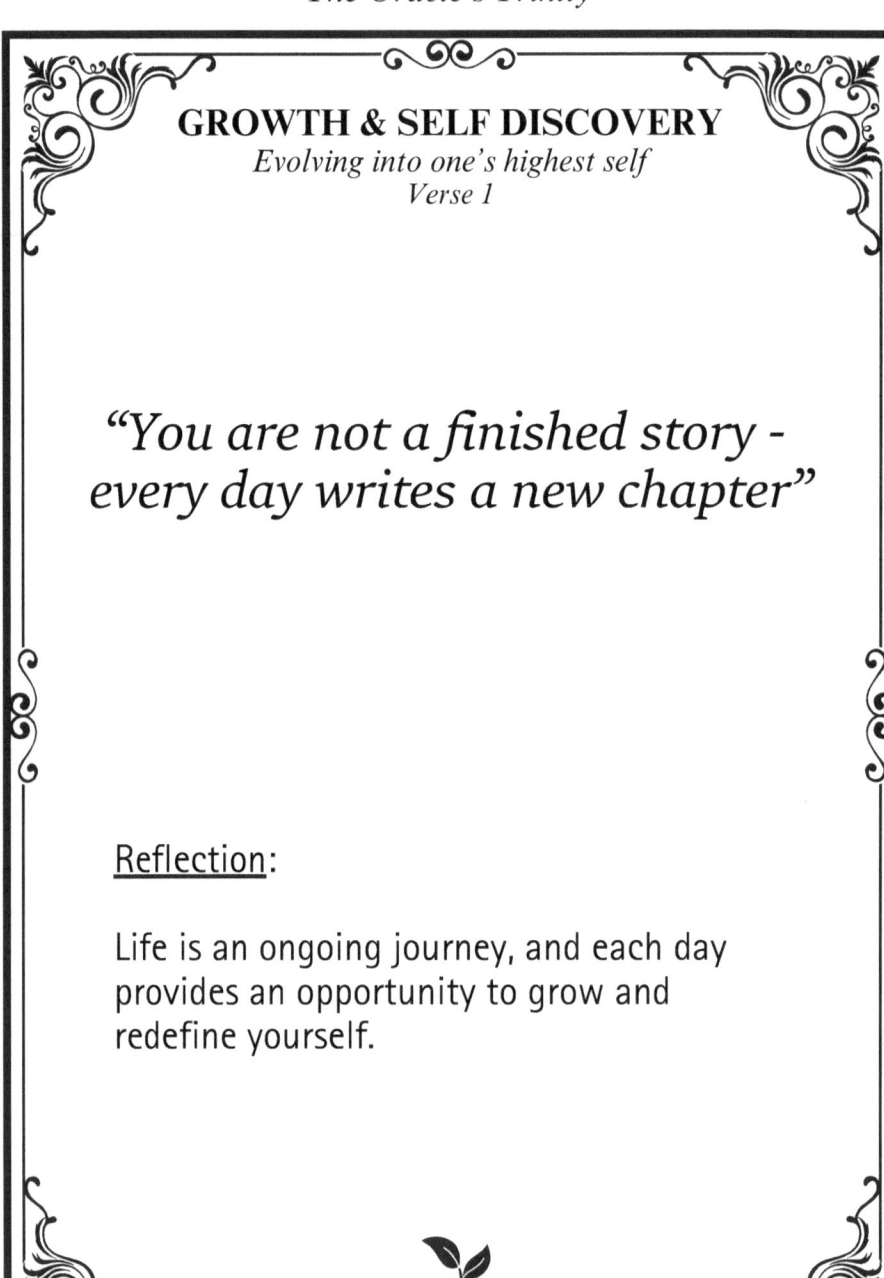

GROWTH & SELF DISCOVERY
Evolving into one's highest self
Verse 1

*"You are not a finished story -
every day writes a new chapter"*

Reflection:

Life is an ongoing journey, and each day
provides an opportunity to grow and
redefine yourself.

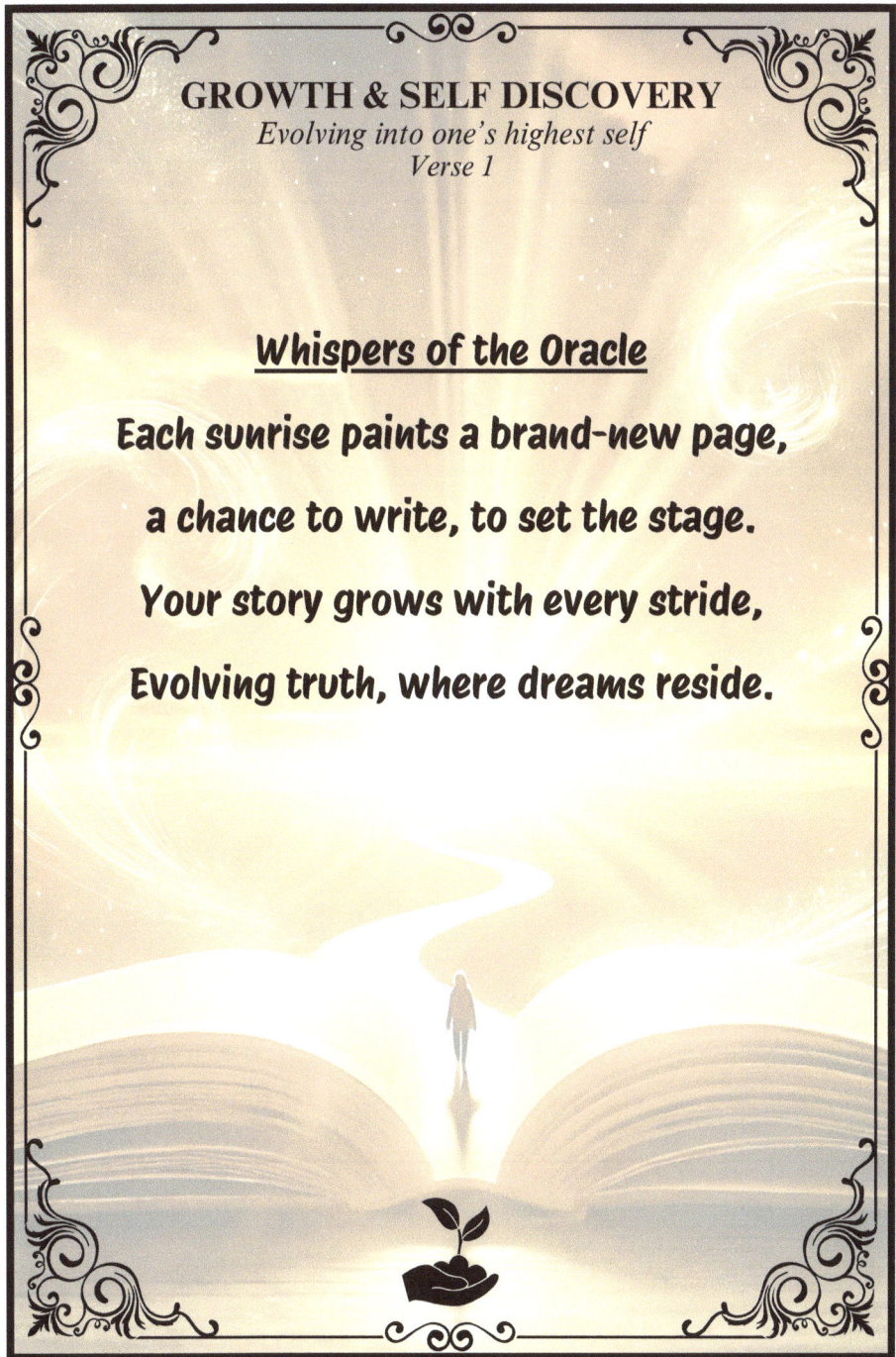

GROWTH & SELF DISCOVERY
Evolving into one's highest self
Verse 1

Whispers of the Oracle

Each sunrise paints a brand-new page,

a chance to write, to set the stage.

Your story grows with every stride,

Evolving truth, where dreams reside.

MOTIVATION & ACTION
Inspiration to move forward
Verse 8

"Motivation may waver, but discipline will carry you through"

Reflection:

Motivation is fleeting, but consistent effort builds lasting success. Prioritize discipline over fleeting feelings.

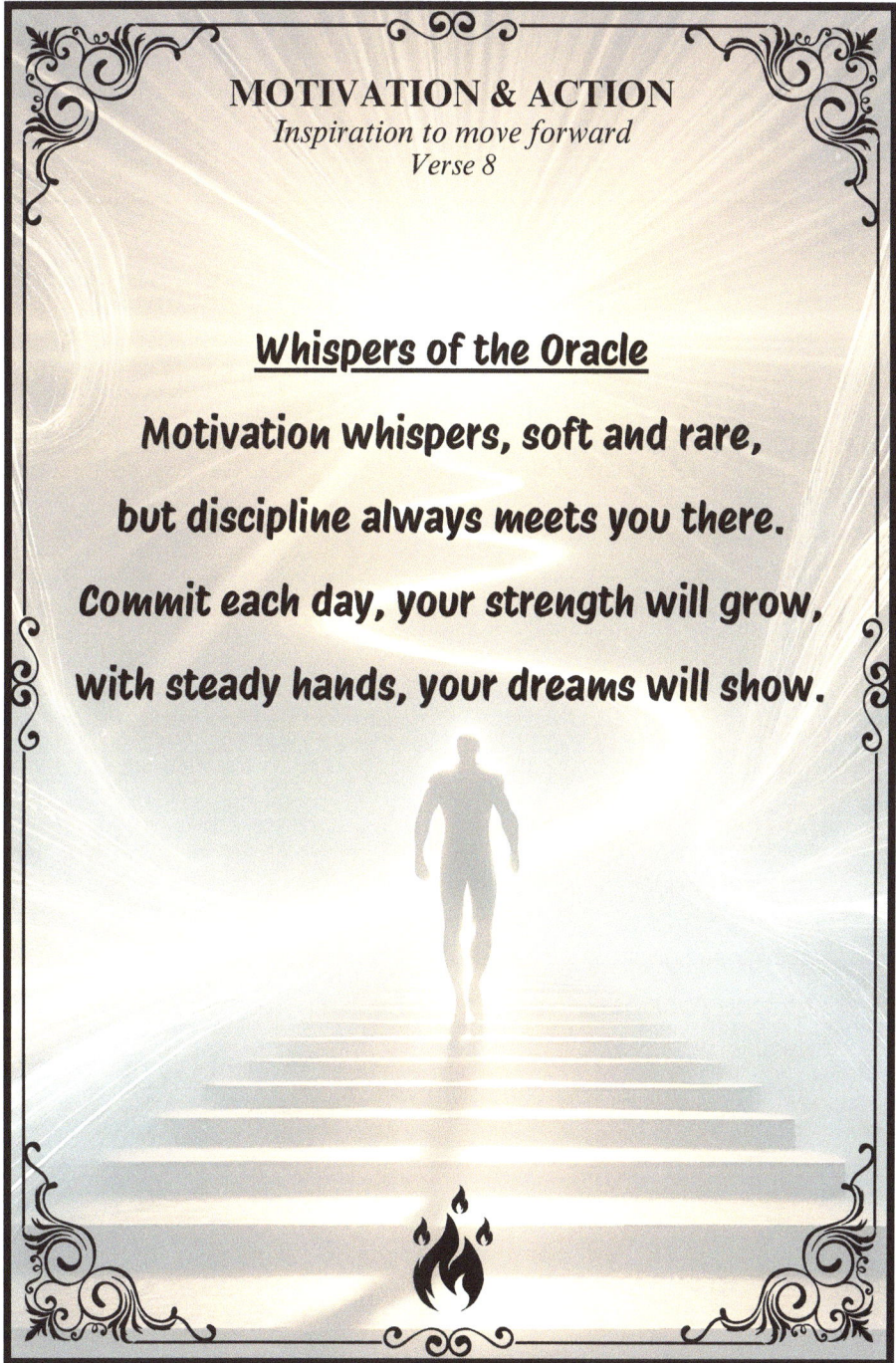

MOTIVATION & ACTION
Inspiration to move forward
Verse 8

Whispers of the Oracle

Motivation whispers, soft and rare,

but discipline always meets you there.

Commit each day, your strength will grow,

with steady hands, your dreams will show.

MOTIVATION & ACTION
Inspiration to move forward
Verse 7

"Every sunrise is a reset button - press it with purpose"

Reflection:

Each day is a fresh start. Use the opportunity to realign with your goals and take meaningful steps forward.

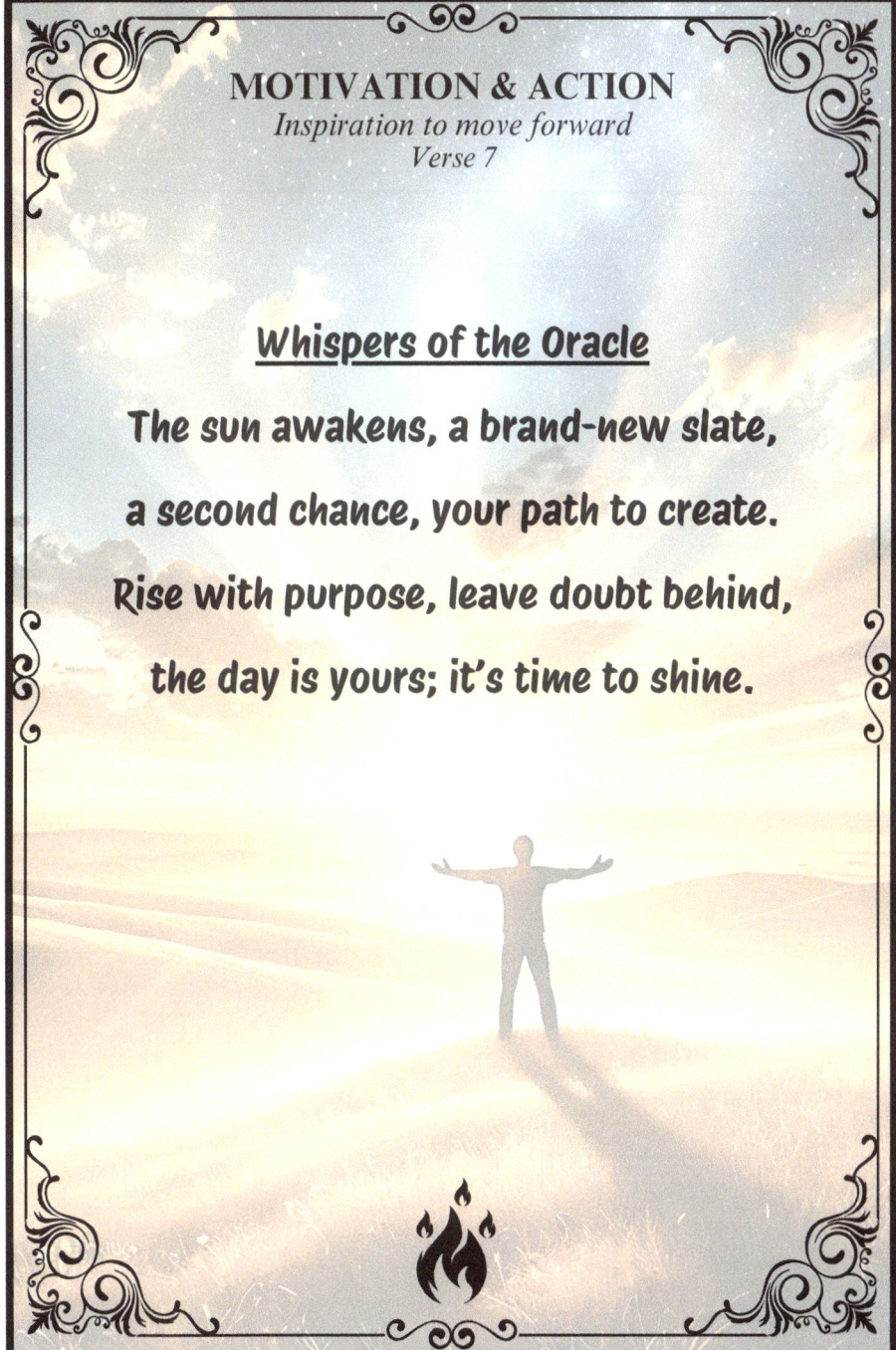

MOTIVATION & ACTION
Inspiration to move forward
Verse 7

<u>Whispers of the Oracle</u>

The sun awakens, a brand-new slate,

a second chance, your path to create.

Rise with purpose, leave doubt behind,

the day is yours; it's time to shine.

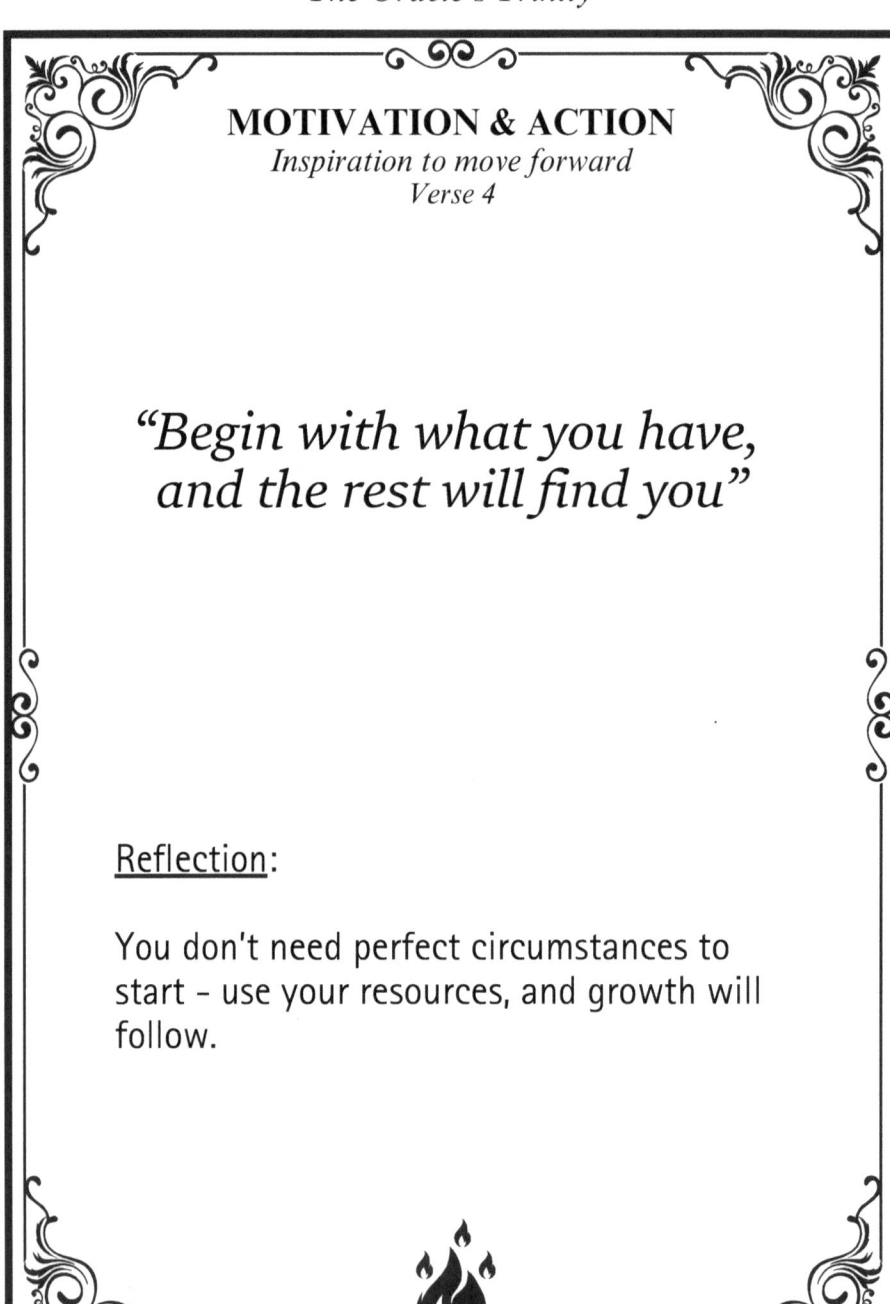

MOTIVATION & ACTION
Inspiration to move forward
Verse 4

"Begin with what you have, and the rest will find you"

Reflection:

You don't need perfect circumstances to start – use your resources, and growth will follow.

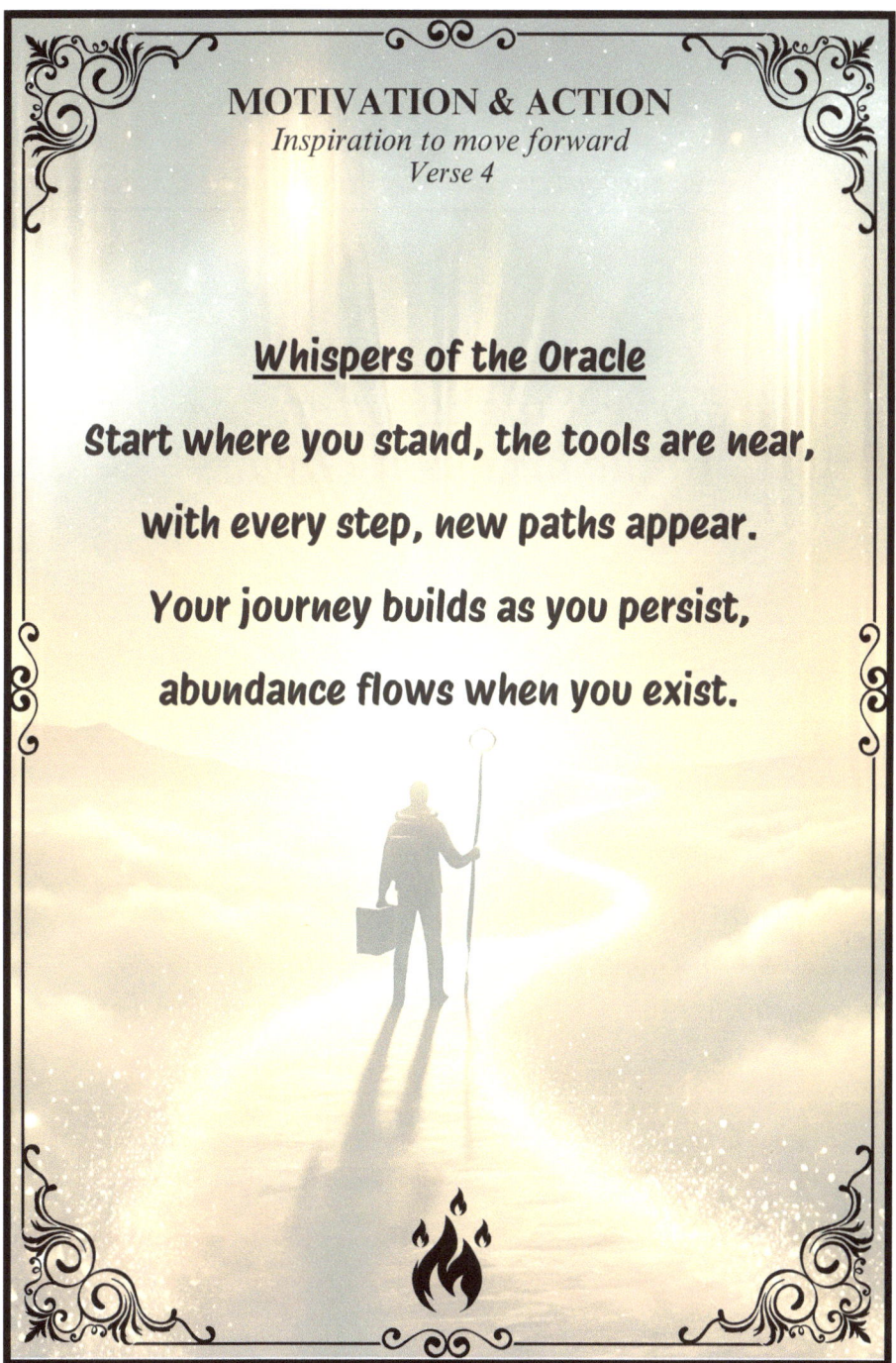

MOTIVATION & ACTION
Inspiration to move forward
Verse 4

<u>Whispers of the Oracle</u>

Start where you stand, the tools are near,

with every step, new paths appear.

Your journey builds as you persist,

abundance flows when you exist.

RESILIENCE & OVERCOMING CHALLENGES
Guidance on Enduring Hardships
Verse 9

"The darkest nights often give birth to the brightest dawns"

Reflection:

Hard times are temporary; they pave the way for new beginnings and brighter moments.

RESILIENCE & OVERCOMING CHALLENGES
Guidance on Enduring Hardships
Verse 9

Whispers of the Oracle

In the darkest nights, a promise lies,

the sun returns to light the skies.

Hold on through shadows, trust the morn,

after every night, a new dawn is born.

RESILIENCE & OVERCOMING CHALLENGES
Guidance on Enduring Hardships
Verse 5

"Every challenge is an invitation to discover your strength"

Reflection:

Life's difficulties are opportunities to realize your full potential. Embrace them as steps toward growth.

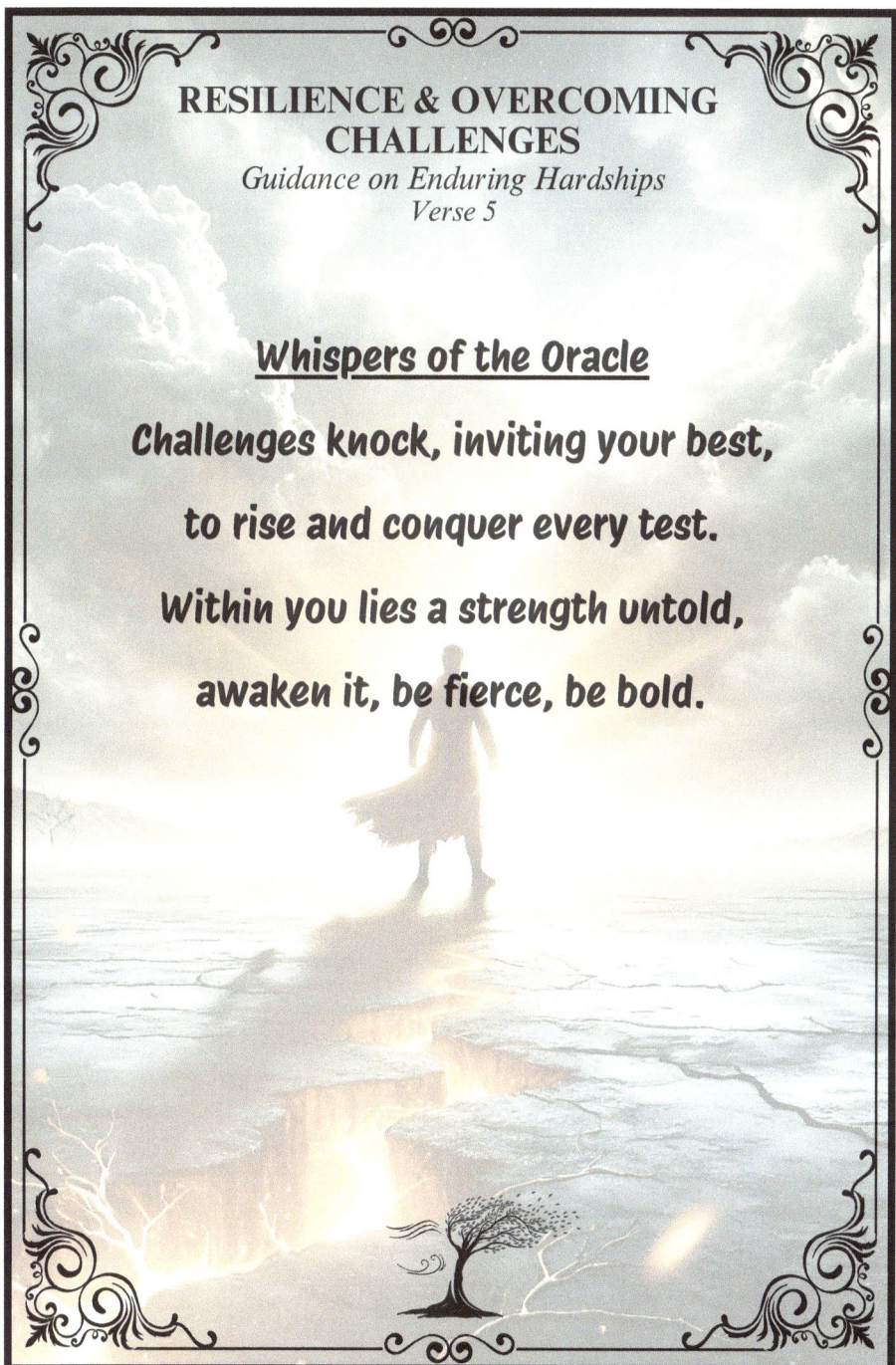

RESILIENCE & OVERCOMING CHALLENGES
Guidance on Enduring Hardships
Verse 5

<u>Whispers of the Oracle</u>

Challenges knock, inviting your best,

to rise and conquer every test.

Within you lies a strength untold,

awaken it, be fierce, be bold.

MOTIVATION & ACTION
Inspiration to move forward
Verse 5

"Excuses are bridges to nowhere; burn them and build roads"

Reflection:

Let go of excuses that hold you back and create pathways to your goals with determination.

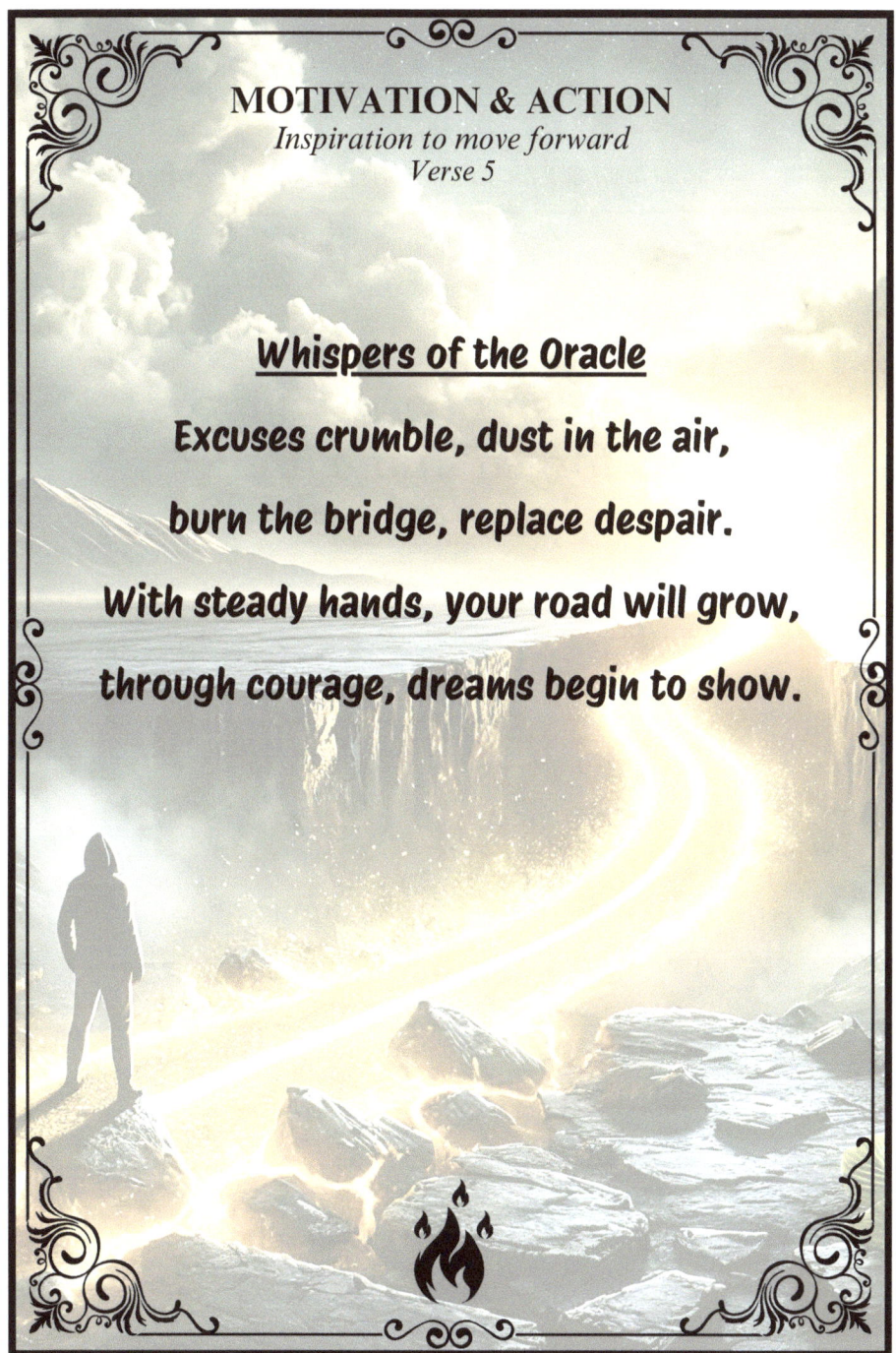

MOTIVATION & ACTION
Inspiration to move forward
Verse 5

Whispers of the Oracle

Excuses crumble, dust in the air,

burn the bridge, replace despair.

With steady hands, your road will grow,

through courage, dreams begin to show.

RESILIENCE & OVERCOMING CHALLENGES
Guidance on Enduring Hardships
Verse 8

"Strength isn't born from ease; it's forged in the fires of persistence"

Reflection:

True strength comes from enduring and overcoming challenges, not avoiding them.

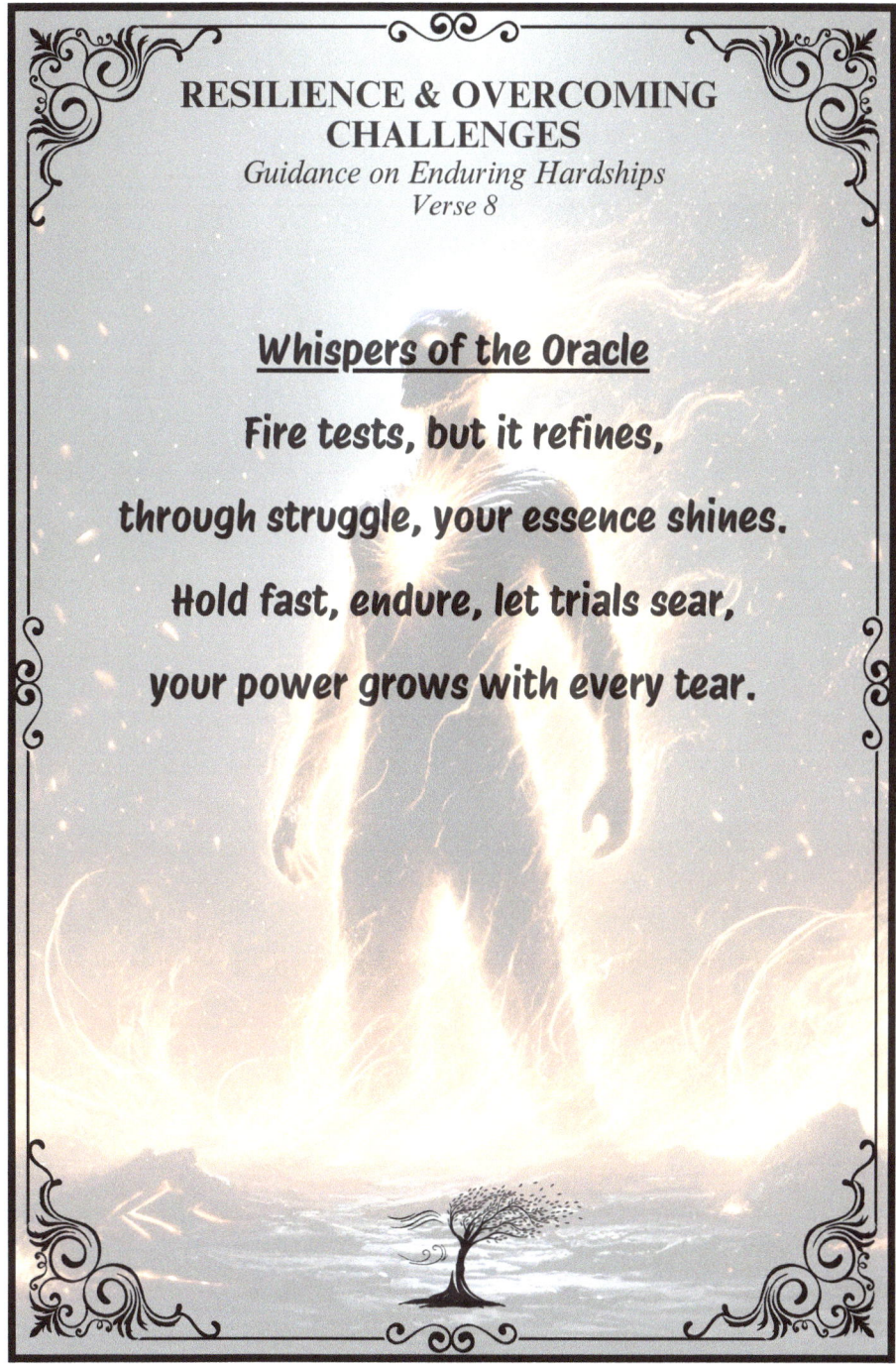

RESILIENCE & OVERCOMING CHALLENGES
Guidance on Enduring Hardships
Verse 8

Whispers of the Oracle

Fire tests, but it refines,

through struggle, your essence shines.

Hold fast, endure, let trials sear,

your power grows with every tear.

MOTIVATION & ACTION
Inspiration to move forward
Verse 9

"Action transforms wishes into reality - start now"

Reflection:

Wishes remain dreams without action. Take the first step to manifest your vision into tangible results.

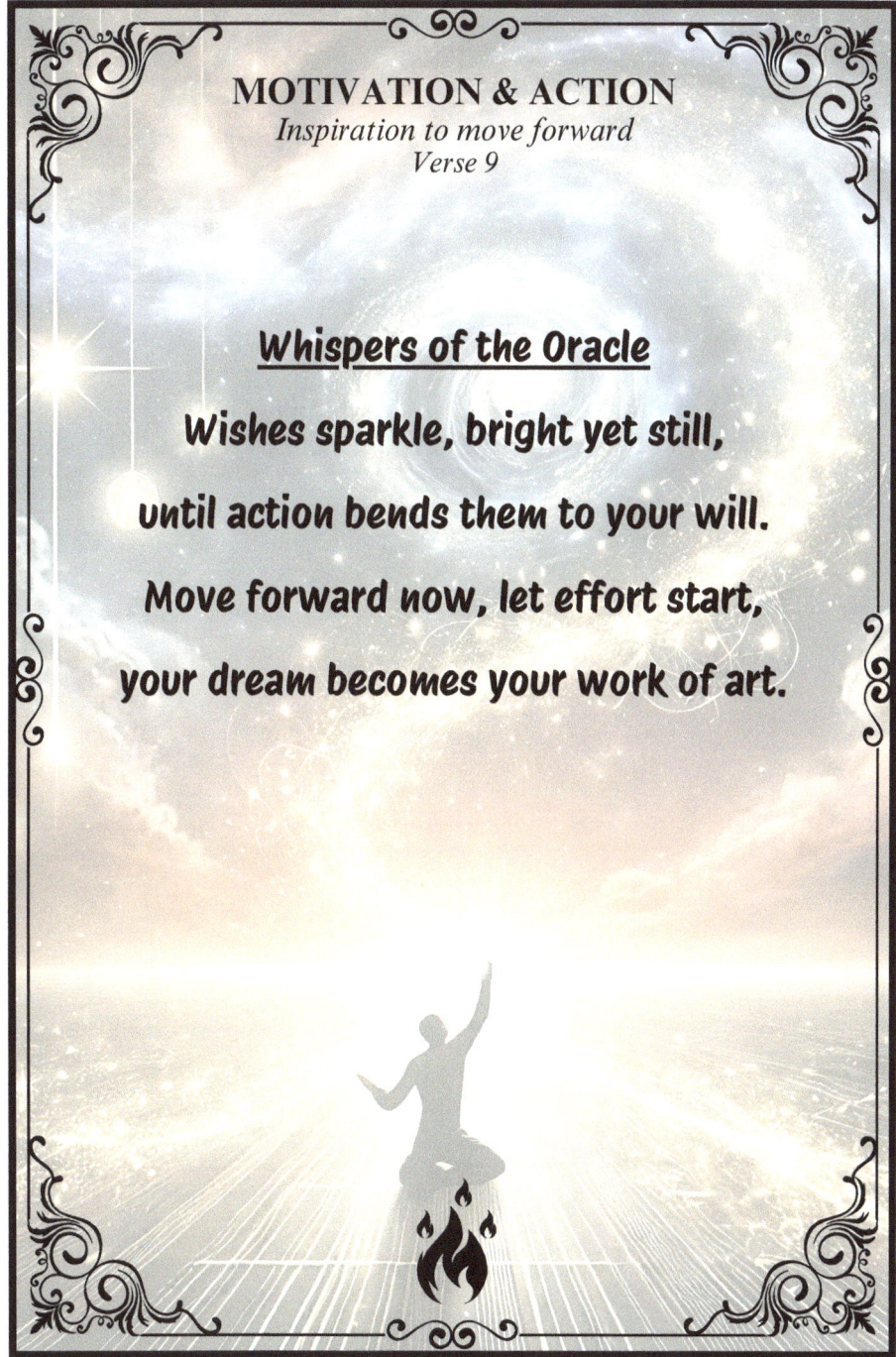

MOTIVATION & ACTION
Inspiration to move forward
Verse 9

Whispers of the Oracle

Wishes sparkle, bright yet still,

until action bends them to your will.

Move forward now, let effort start,

your dream becomes your work of art.

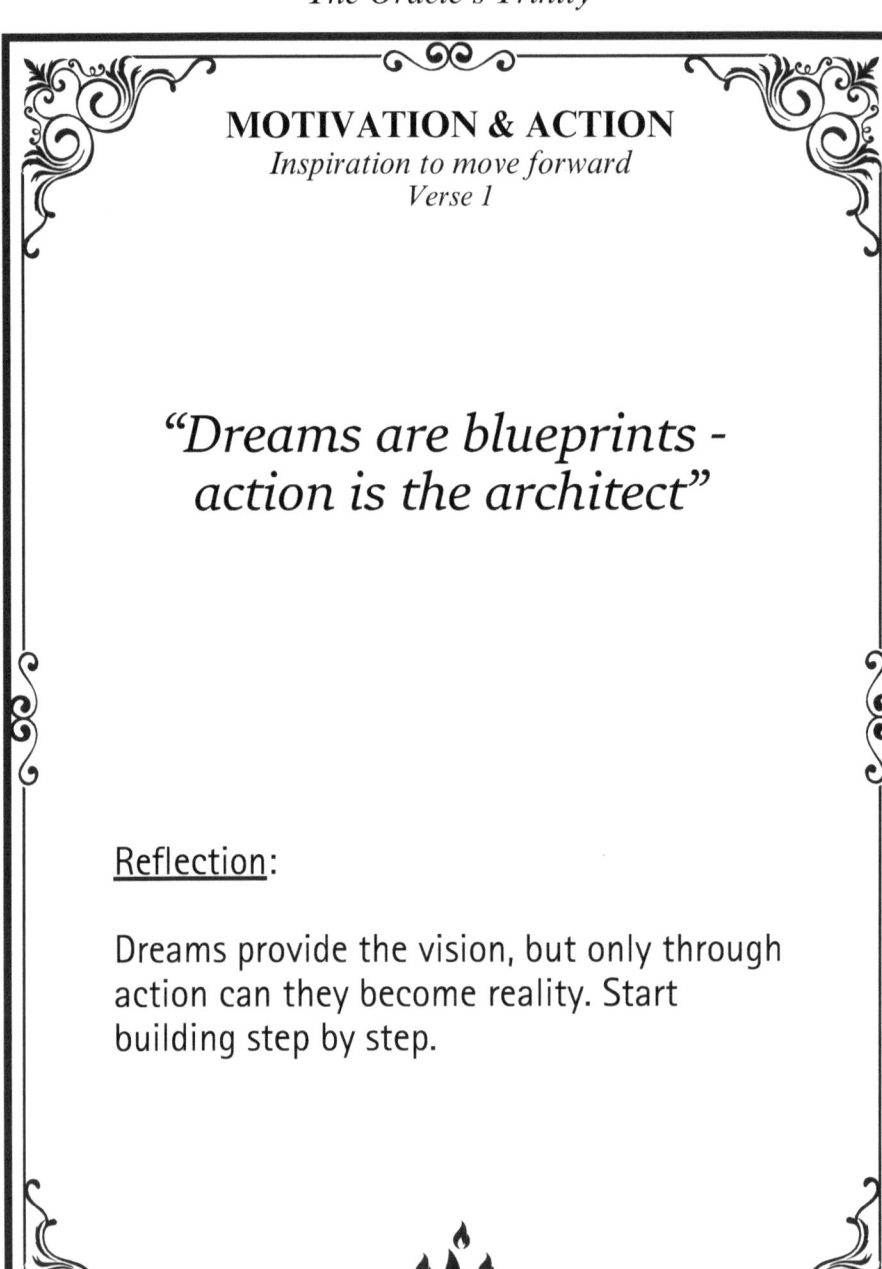

MOTIVATION & ACTION
Inspiration to move forward
Verse 1

"Dreams are blueprints - action is the architect"

Reflection:

Dreams provide the vision, but only through action can they become reality. Start building step by step.

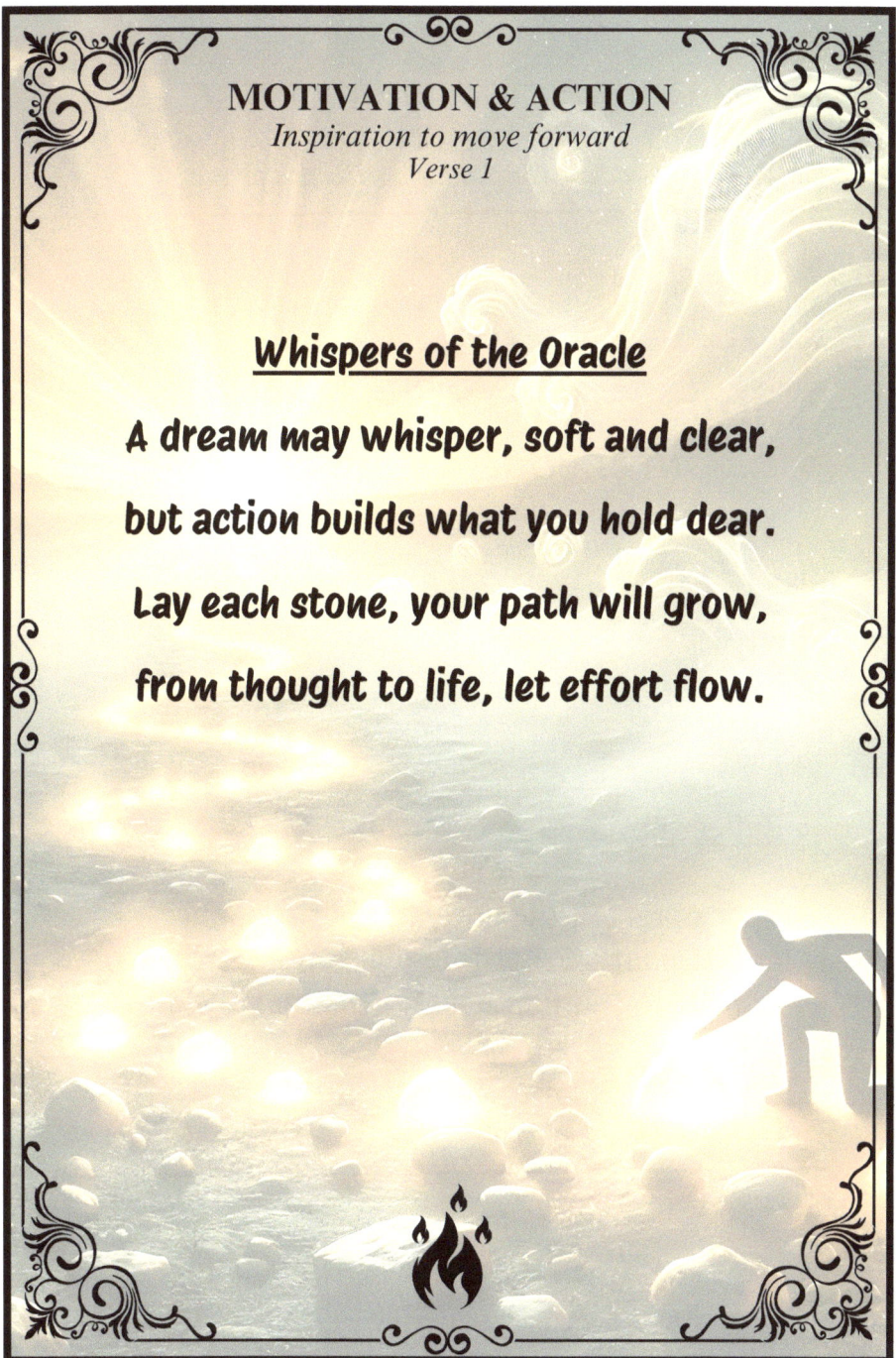

MOTIVATION & ACTION
Inspiration to move forward
Verse 1

Whispers of the Oracle

A dream may whisper, soft and clear,

but action builds what you hold dear.

Lay each stone, your path will grow,

from thought to life, let effort flow.

RESILIENCE & OVERCOMING CHALLENGES
Guidance on Enduring Hardships
Verse 4

"Scars are not marks of failure but medals of survival"

Reflection:

Your scars tell the story of your resilience and strength. Wear them with pride - they symbolize triumph over adversity.

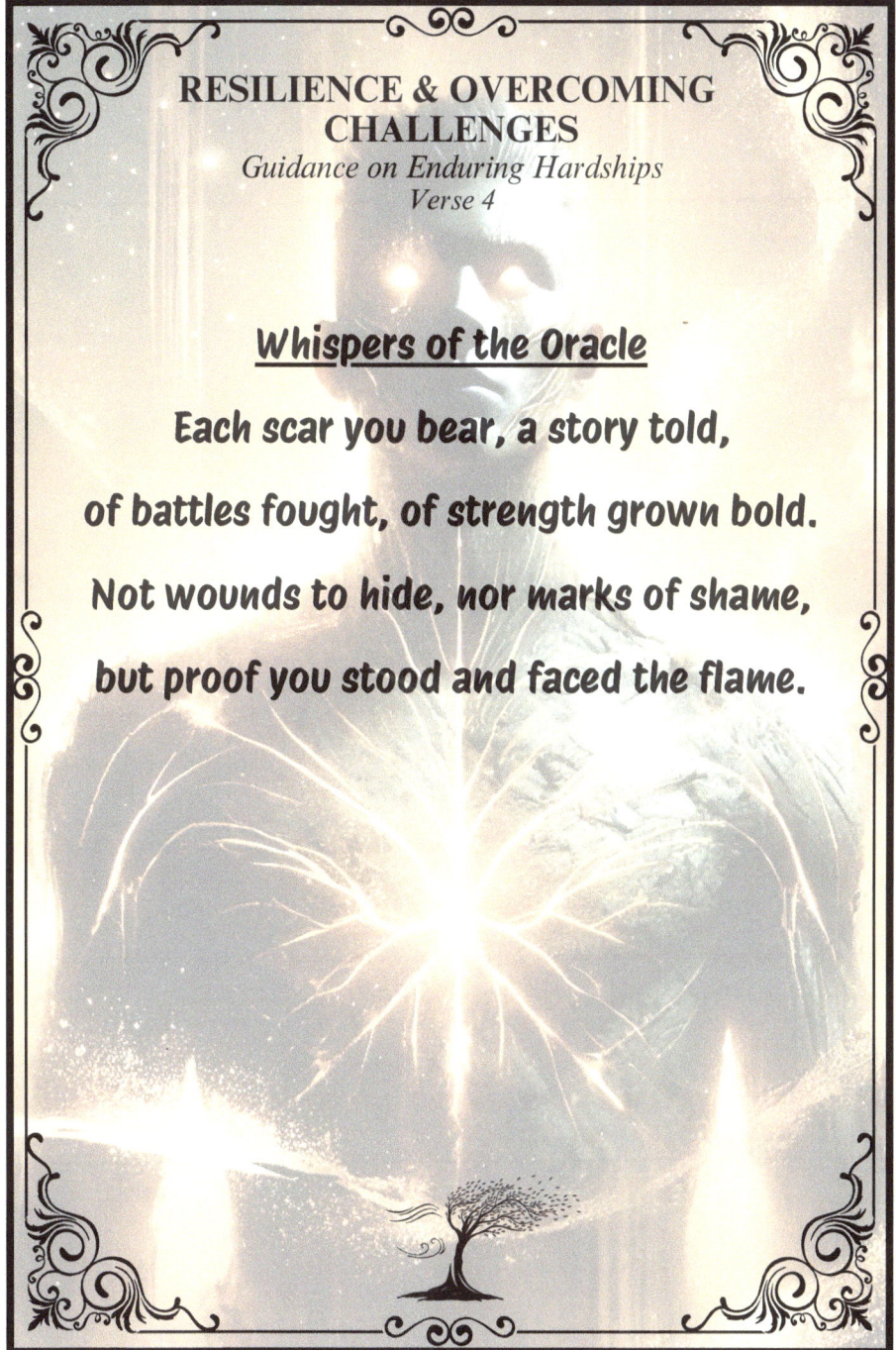

RESILIENCE & OVERCOMING CHALLENGES
Guidance on Enduring Hardships
Verse 4

Whispers of the Oracle

Each scar you bear, a story told,

of battles fought, of strength grown bold.

Not wounds to hide, nor marks of shame,

but proof you stood and faced the flame.

RESILIENCE & OVERCOMING CHALLENGES
Guidance on Enduring Hardships
Verse 1

*"A stumble is not a fall -
it's the universe teaching you
to regain balance"*

Reflection:

Challenges are opportunities to learn and
grow. When you stumble, adjust your
footing and continue forward stronger.

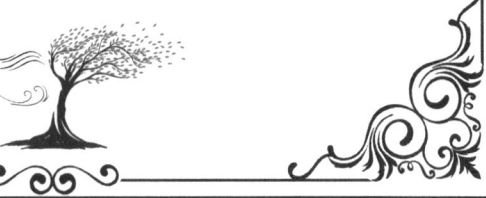

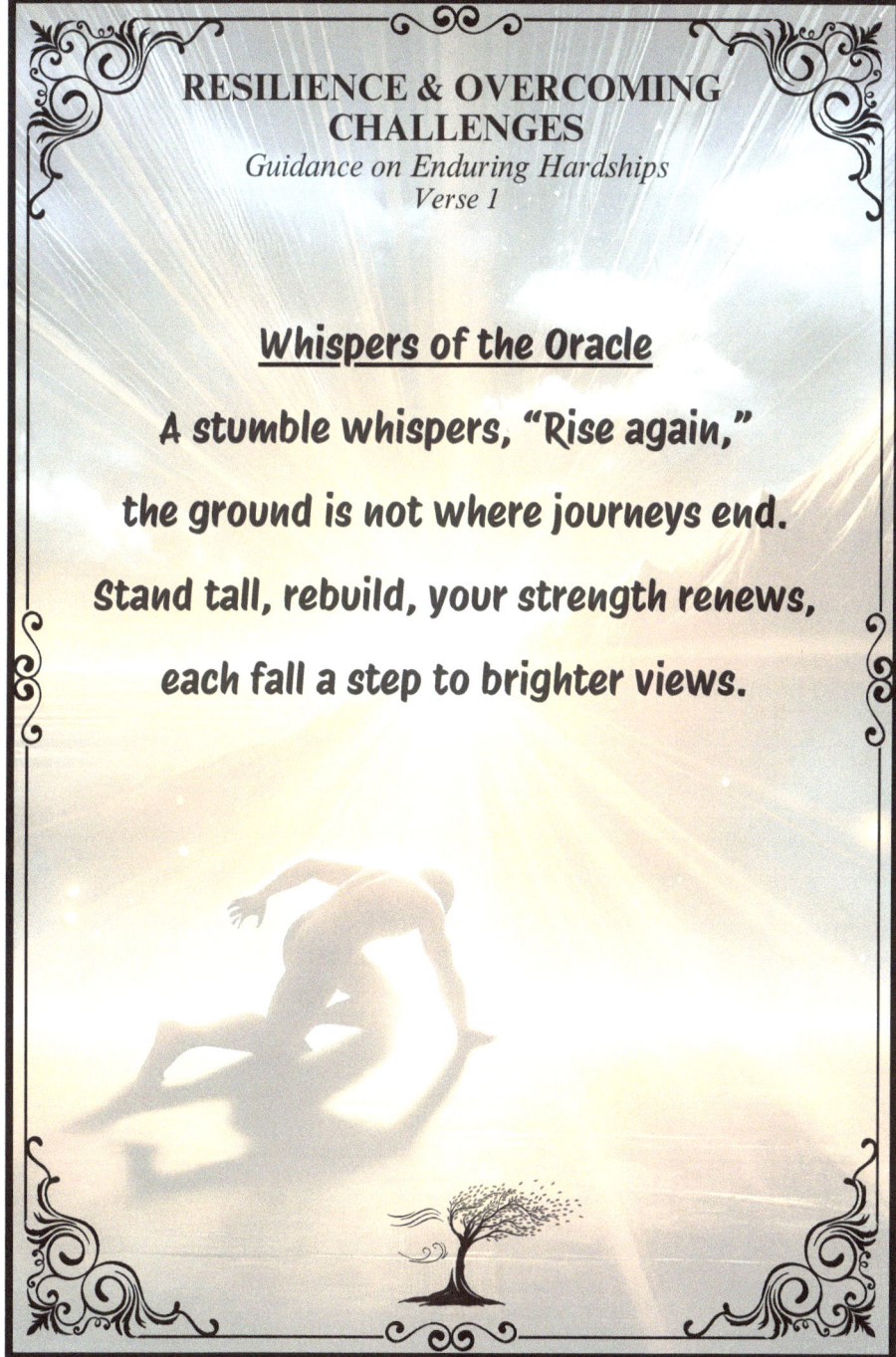

RESILIENCE & OVERCOMING CHALLENGES
Guidance on Enduring Hardships
Verse 1

<u>Whispers of the Oracle</u>

A stumble whispers, "Rise again,"

the ground is not where journeys end.

Stand tall, rebuild, your strength renews,

each fall a step to brighter views.

GROWTH & SELF DISCOVERY
Evolving into one's highest self
Verse 6

"In every mirror, there is a deeper reflection - find it"

<u>Reflection</u>:

Your true self lies beyond surface appearances; take time to explore your inner depths.

GROWTH & SELF DISCOVERY
Evolving into one's highest self
Verse 6

<u>Whispers of the Oracle</u>

The glass reveals, but never all,

dive deeper, answer your heart's call.

Through mirrored depths, your truth will shine,

a light that's endless, yours, divine.

RESILIENCE & OVERCOMING CHALLENGES
Guidance on Enduring Hardships
Verse 2

"In the face of storms, remember: even lightning illuminates the path"

Reflection:

Storms symbolize life's hardships, yet even amidst chaos, there's guidance and clarity to be found.

RESILIENCE & OVERCOMING CHALLENGES
Guidance on Enduring Hardships
Verse 2

Whispers of the Oracle

In thunder's roar; a truth unfolds,

light shines where courage holds.

Through every storm, a path appears,

walk boldly, cast away your fears.

MOTIVATION & ACTION
Inspiration to move forward
Verse 2

"A small step forward is better than a thousand steps imagined"

Reflection:

Progress happens when you act, no matter how small the action. Focus on momentum over perfection.

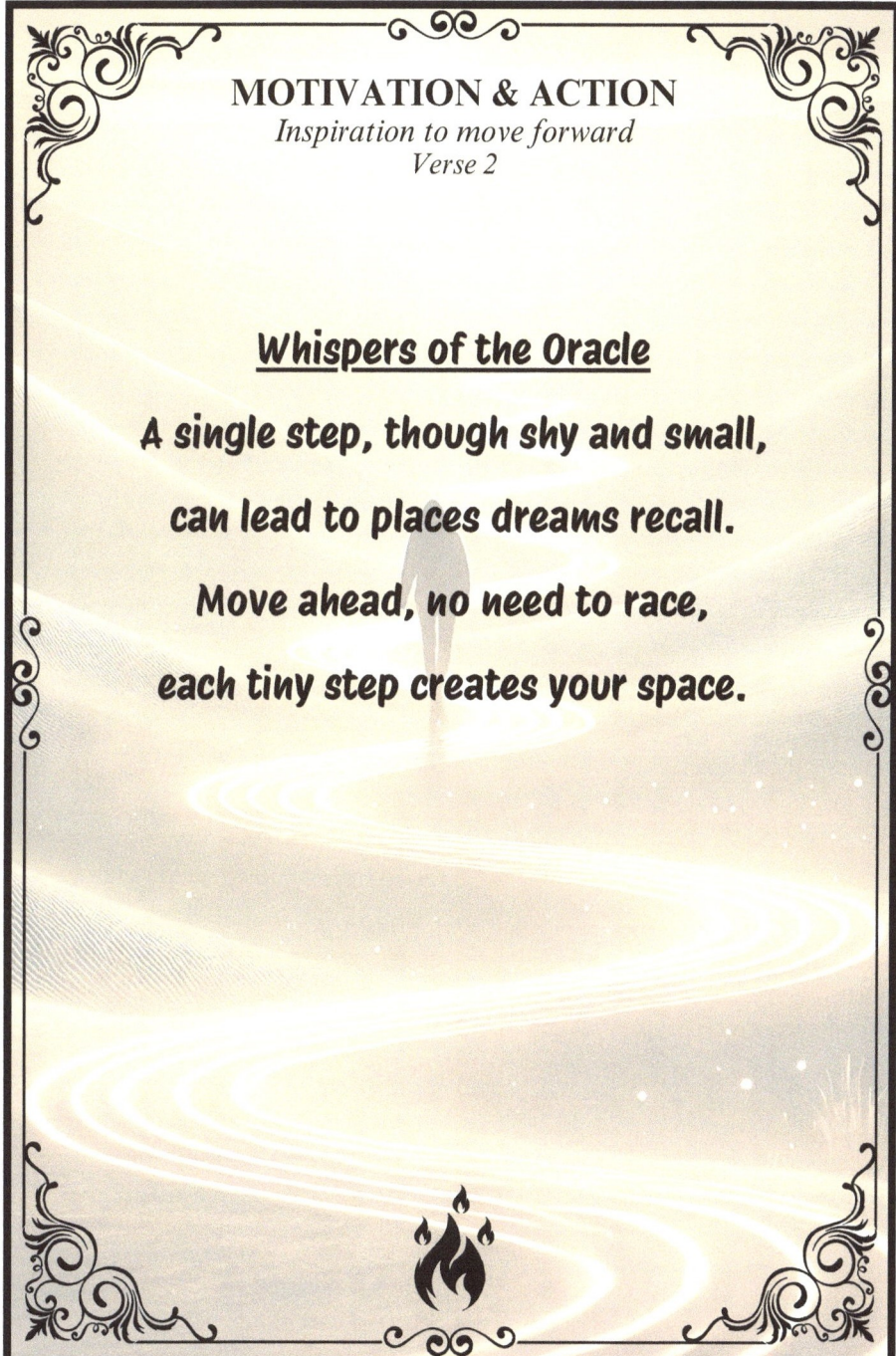

MOTIVATION & ACTION
Inspiration to move forward
Verse 2

<u>Whispers of the Oracle</u>

A single step, though shy and small,

can lead to places dreams recall.

Move ahead, no need to race,

each tiny step creates your space.

GROWTH & SELF DISCOVERY
Evolving into one's highest self
Verse 3

"Your potential is a galaxy - expand into the infinite"

Reflection:

Your capacity for greatness is vast, limited only by the boundaries you set for yourself.

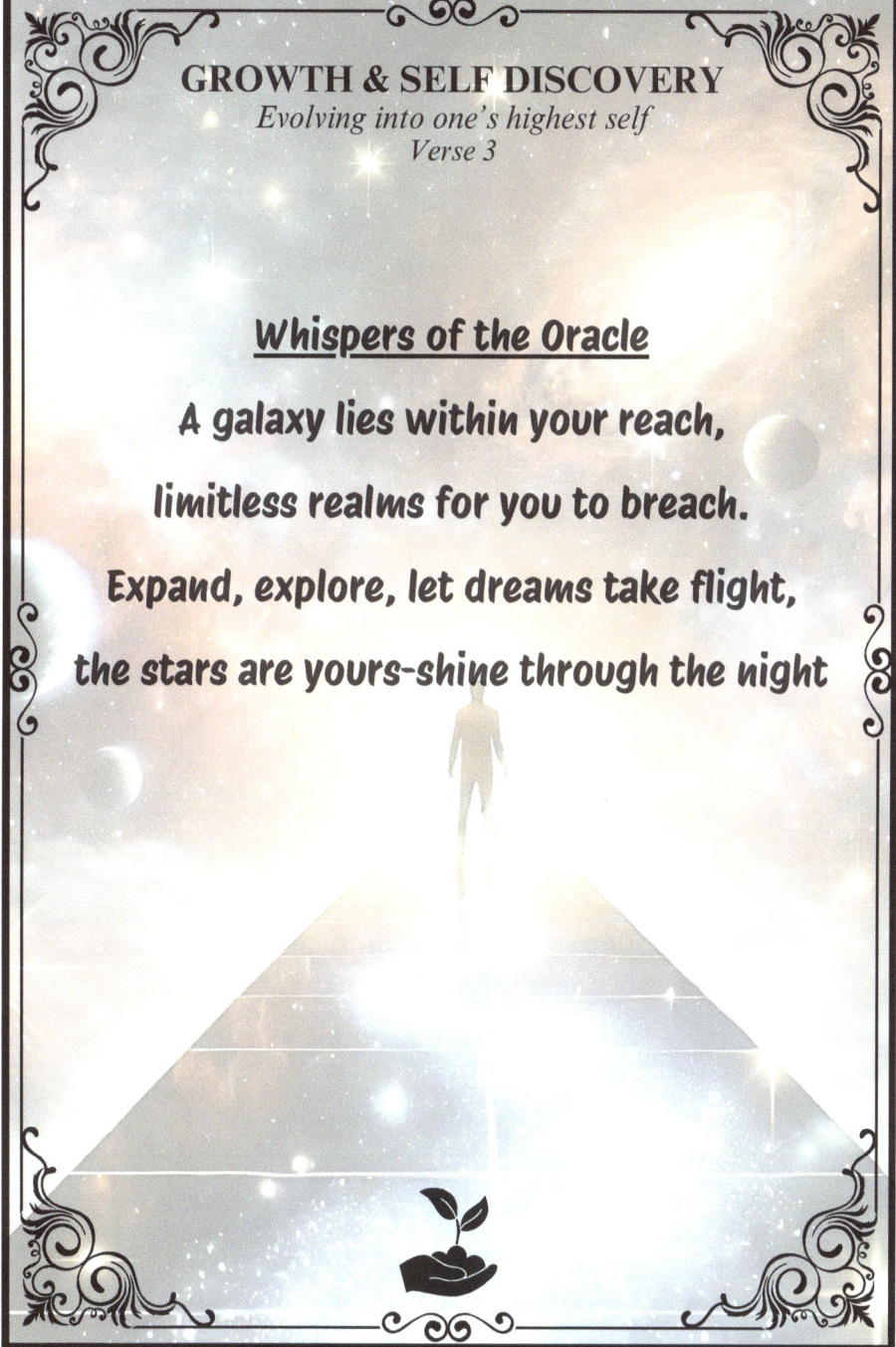

GROWTH & SELF DISCOVERY
Evolving into one's highest self
Verse 3

<u>Whispers of the Oracle</u>

A galaxy lies within your reach,

limitless realms for you to breach.

Expand, explore, let dreams take flight,

the stars are yours-shine through the night

GROWTH & SELF DISCOVERY
Evolving into one's highest self
Verse 4

"Curiosity is the compass of discovery; follow it without fear"

Reflection:

Embrace your curiosity - it leads to new opportunities, knowledge, and personal growth.

GROWTH & SELF DISCOVERY
Evolving into one's highest self
Verse 4

Whispers of the Oracle

Curiosity whispers, "Come and see,"

a map of wonders, wild and free.

Follow the pull, let courage steer,

discovery awaits, so hold no fear.

RESILIENCE & OVERCOMING CHALLENGES
Guidance on Enduring Hardships
Verse 7

"The climb is steepest before the peek - hold steady and rise"

Reflection:

The hardest moments come just before a breakthrough. Stay focused and keep moving forward.

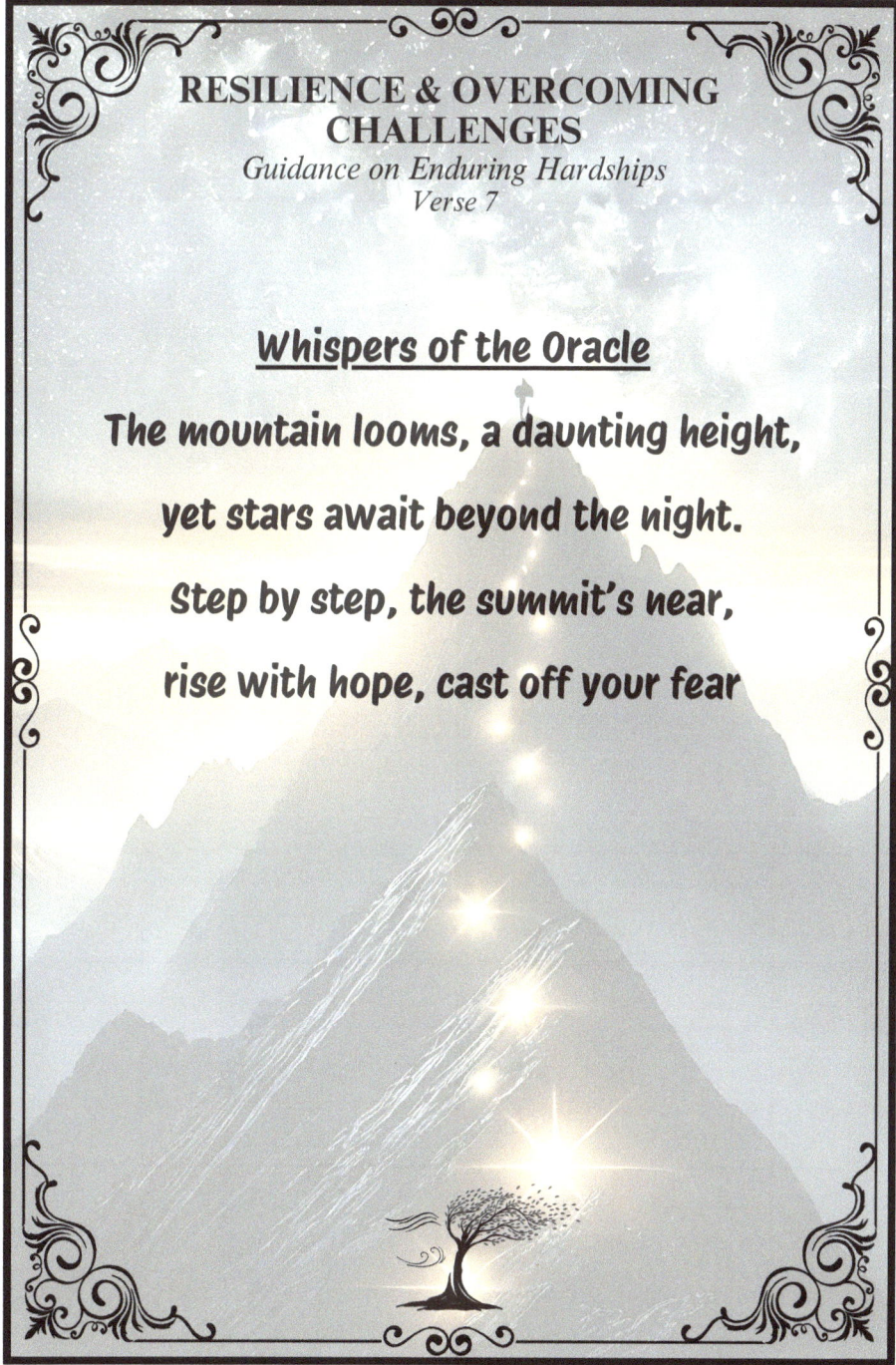

RESILIENCE & OVERCOMING CHALLENGES
Guidance on Enduring Hardships
Verse 7

Whispers of the Oracle

The mountain looms, a daunting height,

yet stars await beyond the night.

Step by step, the summit's near,

rise with hope, cast off your fear

RESILIENCE & OVERCOMING CHALLENGES
Guidance on Enduring Hardships
Verse 6

"Adversity is a sculptor, shaping the masterpiece within you"

Reflection:

Hardships refine your character and mold you into a stronger, more resilient person.

RESILIENCE & OVERCOMING CHALLENGES
Guidance on Enduring Hardships
Verse 6

<u>Whispers of the Oracle</u>

Adversity carves, with steady hands,

a masterpiece that firmly stands.

Let every trial shape your form,

through storms, your spirit is reborn

MOTIVATION & ACTION
Inspiration to move forward
Verse 3

"The world moves for those who refuse to stand still"

Reflection:

Momentum attracts opportunity. Keep moving, and life will open doors you didn't expect.

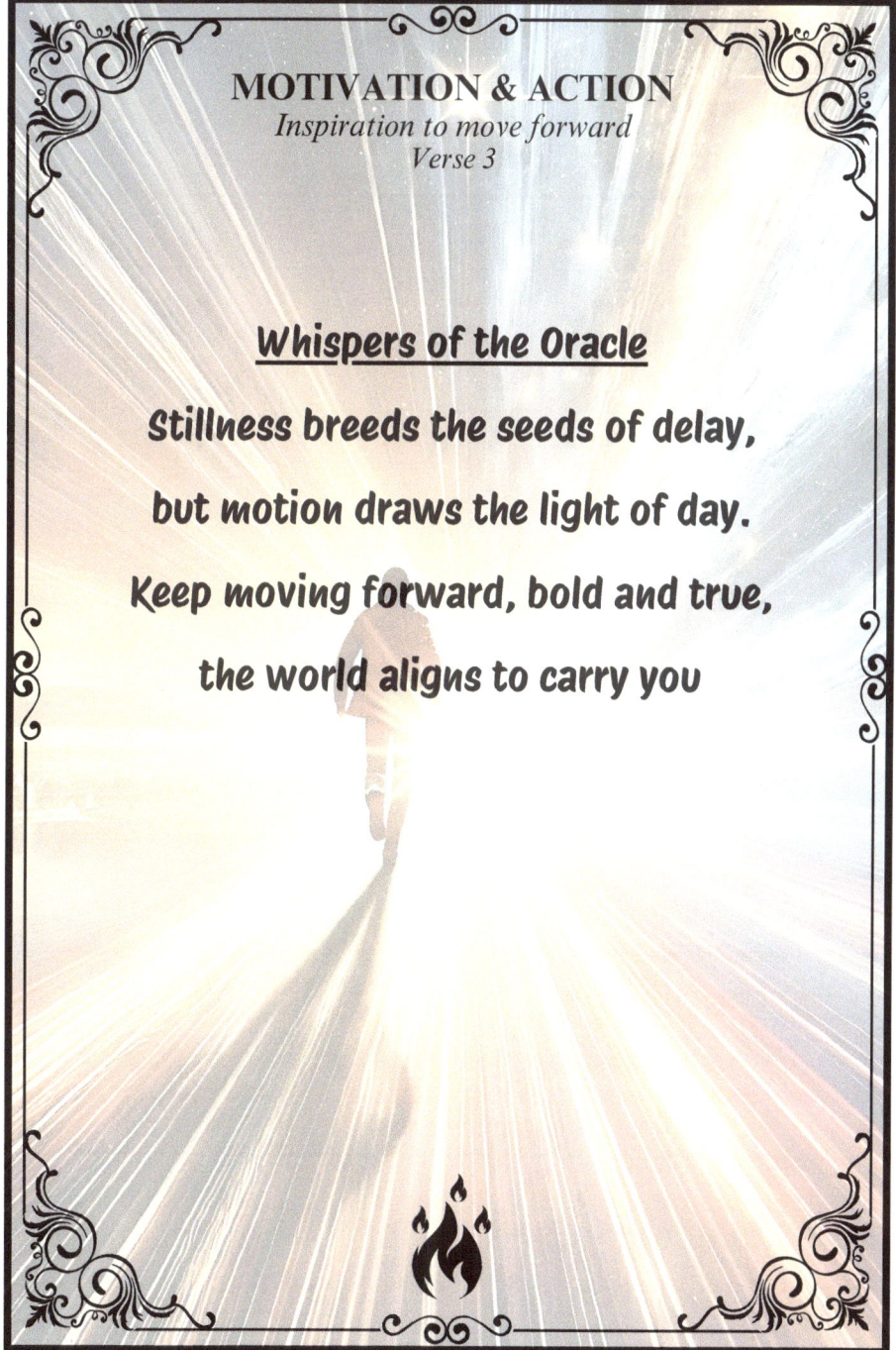

MOTIVATION & ACTION
Inspiration to move forward
Verse 3

Whispers of the Oracle

Stillness breeds the seeds of delay,

but motion draws the light of day.

Keep moving forward, bold and true,

the world aligns to carry you

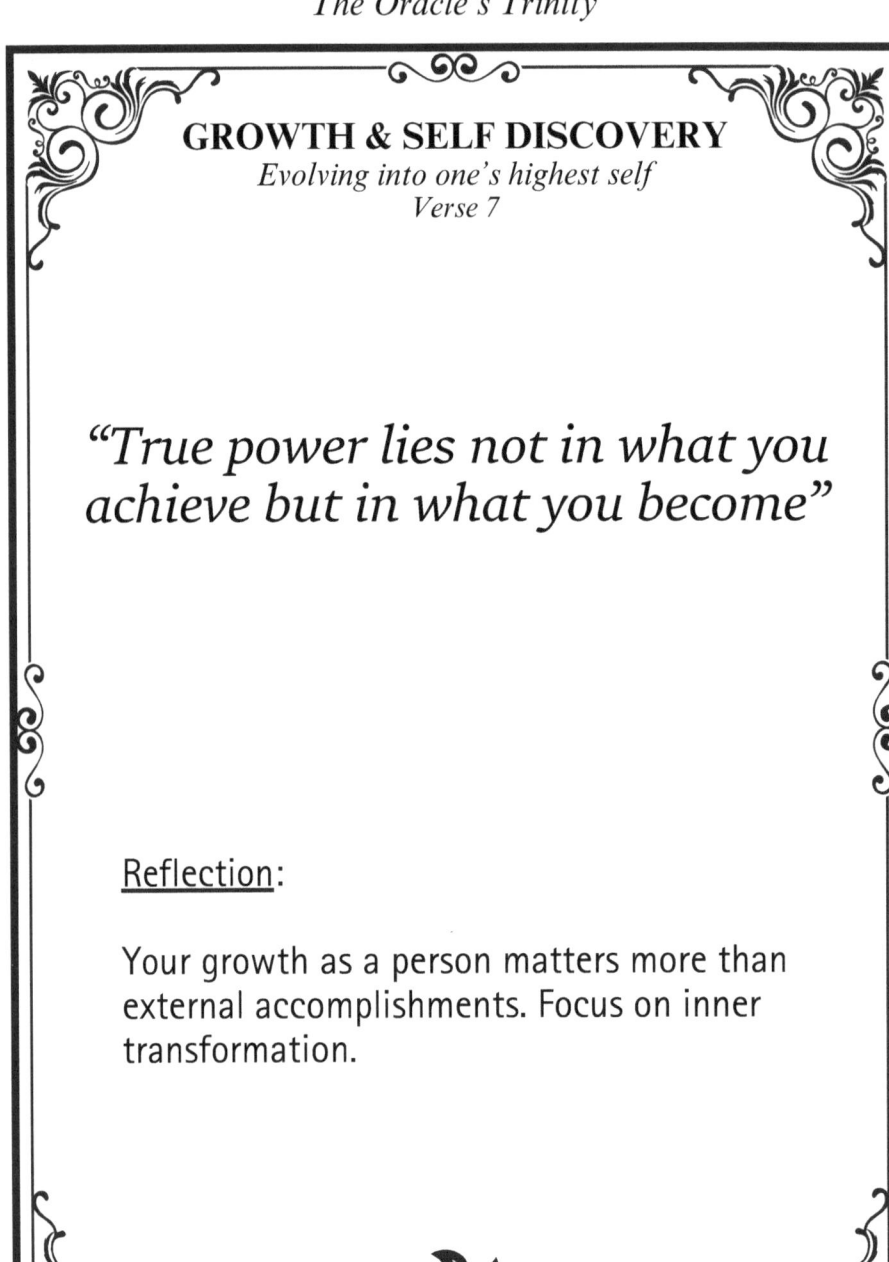

GROWTH & SELF DISCOVERY
Evolving into one's highest self
Verse 7

"True power lies not in what you achieve but in what you become"

Reflection:

Your growth as a person matters more than external accomplishments. Focus on inner transformation.

GROWTH & SELF DISCOVERY
Evolving into one's highest self
Verse 7

Whispers of the Oracle

The heights you reach, the world may see,

but greater still, who you will be.

Through trials forged, your essence glows,

inward change, where true strength flows

GROWTH & SELF DISCOVERY
Evolving into one's highest self
Verse 8

"Growth begins at the edge of your comfort zone - step boldly"

Reflection:

Progress requires leaving your comfort zone. Embrace discomfort as a sign of transformation.

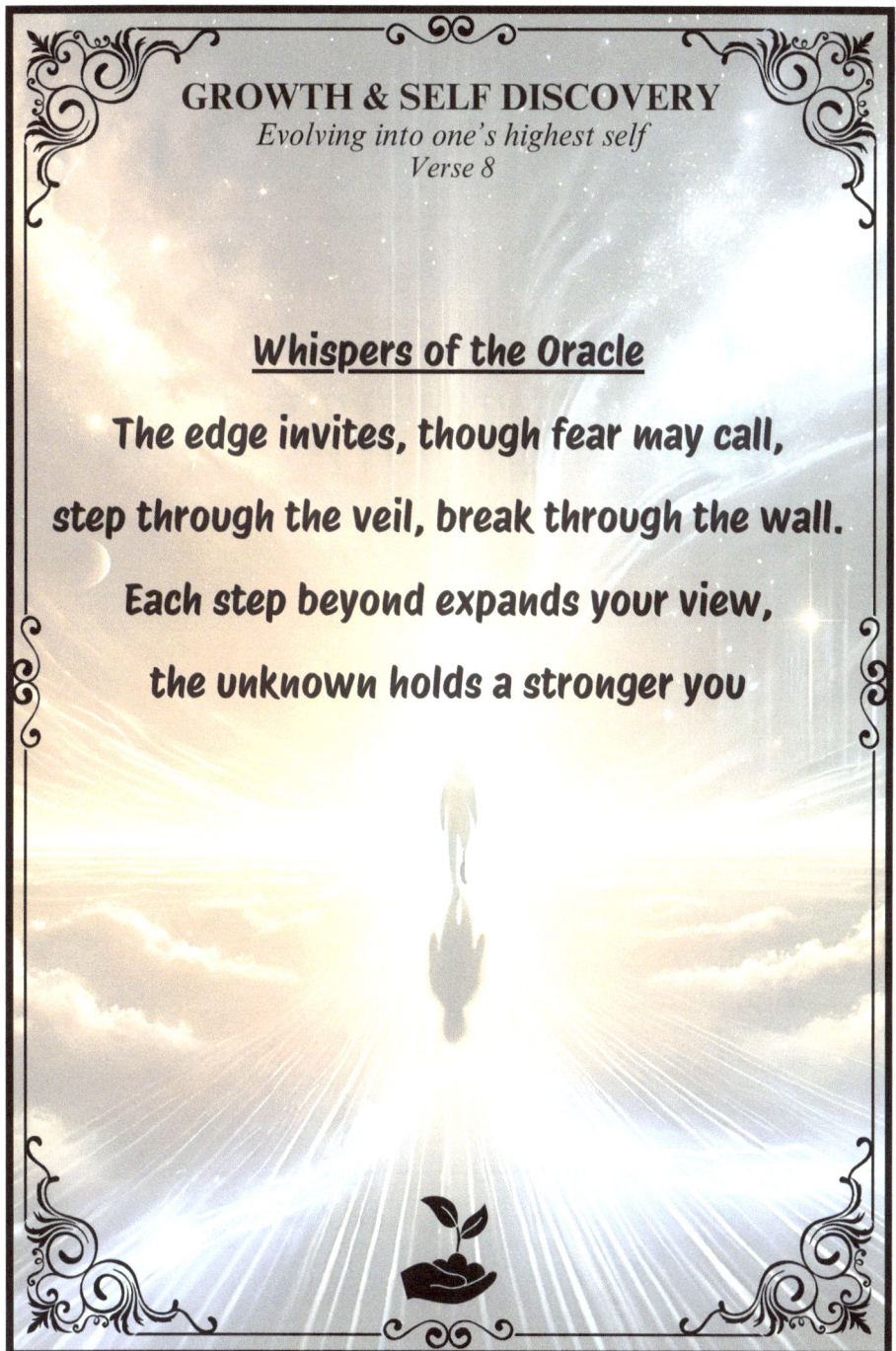

GROWTH & SELF DISCOVERY
Evolving into one's highest self
Verse 8

Whispers of the Oracle

The edge invites, though fear may call,

step through the veil, break through the wall.

Each step beyond expands your view,

the unknown holds a stronger you

GROWTH & SELF DISCOVERY
Evolving into one's highest self
Verse 2

"The roots of growth are hidden, but their fruits feed the world"

Reflection:

The most profound personal growth happens below the surface, unseen but impactful.

GROWTH & SELF DISCOVERY
Evolving into one's highest self
Verse 2

Whispers of the Oracle

Beneath the soil, unseen, unknown,

roots dig deep, and strength is sown.

In time, the fruits of labor show,

a towering tree, where dreams can grow

Thematic Guide

Book 1: Strength of the Oracle's Trinity contains three Oracle categories:

1) Resilience and Overcoming Challenges

2) Growth and Self-Discovery

3) Motivation and Action

While these messages are woven together for an intuitive experience, you may wish to seek wisdom from a specific category. Use this guide to find the path you need in this moment.

Refer to the next page for the page number of each verse for each category.

Thematic Guide

Category 1: Resilience and Overcoming Challenges
(Guidance on enduring hardship)

Verse 1: pp.31–32	Verse 4: pp.29–30	Verse 7: pp.43–44
Verse 2: pp.35–36	Verse 5: pp.19–20	Verse 8: pp.23–24
Verse 3: pp.7–8	Verse 6: pp.45–46	Verse 9: pp.17–18

Category 2: Growth and Self-Discovery
(Evolving into one's highest self)

Verse 1: pp.9–10	Verse 4: pp.41–42	Verse 7: pp.49–50
Verse 2: pp.53–54	Verse 5: pp.3–4	Verse 8: pp.51–52
Verse 3: pp.39–40	Verse 6: pp.33–34	Verse 9: pp.1–2

Category 3: Motivation and Action
(Inspiration to move forward)

Verse 1: pp.27–28	Verse 4: pp.15–16	Verse 7: pp.13–14
Verse 2: pp.37–38	Verse 5: pp.21–22	Verse 8: pp.11–12
Verse 3: pp.47–48	Verse 6: pp.5–6	Verse 9: pp.25–26

Continue Your Journey

This book is part of The Oracle's Trinity, a collection of 3 Oracle books, consisting of:

Book 1: Strength – The Oracle of Resilience, Growth, and Action

Book 2: Harmony - The Oracle of Love, Inner Peace, and Purpose

Book 3: Hope - The Oracle of Courage, Vision, and Infinite Possibilities

At the time of this book's publication, Book 2 and Book 3 are still being prepared. The Oracle's Trinity is curated and presented by Something Nice, LLC. Information on future release and additional offerings:

Website Coming Soon: www.somethingnicehawaii.com
For Inquiries, email: contact@somethingnicehawaii.com

- Notes -

- Notes -

- Notes -

- Notes -

- Notes -

- Notes -

www.ingramcontent.com/pod-product-compliance
Lightning Source LLC
Chambersburg PA
CBHW041729240626
47171CB00001B/3